HYDROPONIC HIJINKS

Don't Miss Any of Astrid's
Out-of-This-World Adventures!

The Astronomically Grand Plan

The Unlucky Launch

Hydroponic Hijinks

ASTRID THE ASTRONAUT

HYDROPONIC HIJINKS

By Rie Neal ★ Illustrated by Talitha Shipman

ALADDIN
New York   London   Toronto   Sydney   New Delhi

This book is a work of fiction. Any references to historical events, real people, or real places are used fictitiously. Other names, characters, places, and events are products of the author's imagination, and any resemblance to actual events or places or persons, living or dead, is entirely coincidental.

ALADDIN • An imprint of Simon & Schuster Children's Publishing Division • 1230 Avenue of the Americas, New York, New York 10020 • First Aladdin paperback edition October 2022 • Text copyright © 2022 by Rie Neal • Illustrations copyright © 2022 by Talitha Shipman • Also available in an Aladdin hardcover edition. • All rights reserved, including the right of reproduction in whole or in part in any form. • ALADDIN and related logo are registered trademarks of Simon & Schuster, Inc. • For information about special discounts for bulk purchases, please contact Simon & Schuster Special Sales at 1-866-506-1949 or business@simonandschuster.com. • The Simon & Schuster Speakers Bureau can bring authors to your live event. For more information or to book an event contact the Simon & Schuster Speakers Bureau at 1-866-248-3049 or visit our website at www.simonspeakers.com. • Book designed by Laura Lyn DiSiena • The illustrations for this book were rendered digitally. • The text of this book was set in Ionic No 5. • Manufactured in the United States of America 0922 OFF • 2 4 6 8 10 9 7 5 3 1 • Library of Congress Cataloging-in-Publication Data • Names: Neal, Rie, author. | Shipman, Talitha, illustrator. • Title: Hydroponic hijinks / by Rie Neal ; illustrated by Talitha Shipman. • Description: First Aladdin paperback edition. | New York : Aladdin, 2022. | Series: Astrid the astronaut ; book 3 | Audience: Ages 6 to 9. | Summary: When members of the Shooting Stars and Petite Picassos team up for a combined STEM and art project, Astrid is torn between her best friend, Hallie, and her archrival, Pearl, until she overcomes her initial suspicions and realizes being a good teammate is more about working together than winning. • Identifiers: LCCN 2022009775 (print) | LCCN 2022009776 (ebook) | ISBN 9781534481541 (hardcover) | ISBN 9781534481534 (paperback) | ISBN 9781534481558 (ebook) • Subjects: CYAC: After-school programs—Fiction. | Clubs—Fiction. | Cooperativeness—Fiction. | Hearing impaired—Fiction. | LCGFT: Novels. • Classification: LCC PZ7.1.N3826 Hy 2022 (print) | LCC PZ7.1.N3826 (ebook) | DDC [Fic]—dc23 • LC record available at https://lccn.loc.gov/2022009775 • LC ebook record available at https://lccn.loc.gov/2022009776

FOR MOM AND DAD

—R. N.

TO CORAL,

MY AWESOME ASTRONAUT

—T. S.

CONTENTS

CHAPTER 1: *A GREAT TEAMMATE*   1

CHAPTER 2: *THE BEST SURPRISE EVER*   9

CHAPTER 3: *MISSION: CONTROL*   19

CHAPTER 4: *SPROUTS*   31

CHAPTER 5: *PROBLEMS WITH PEARL*   44

CHAPTER 6: *CIRCUIT BOARDS AND SOCCER BALLS*   54

CHAPTER 7: *SOMETHING SMELLS*   59

CHAPTER 8: *SPYING*   65

CHAPTER 9: *PEARL'S SECRET*   71

CHAPTER 10: *PART OF THE TEAM*   78

⋆ CHAPTER 1 ⋆

A GREAT TEAMMATE

"**O**ver here!" I shouted. My feet flew through the grass. I slid a finger behind my hearing aids to get rid of the sweat there.

My best friend, Hallie, nodded. She slammed the soccer ball over to me.

A kid from the other team ran up, and I pivoted to block the ball.

This shot was *mine*.

With short kicks, I dodged around him. But he wasn't giving up. He stuck a hand out to throw me off, but I twirled around it.

Veejay, my other best friend, ran up. Two kids from the other team were right behind him. "Astrid!" he panted. "Pearl is open!"

He was right. Pearl stood in front of the goal, waving her arms.

We'd been playing soccer every recess this week, and I was getting really good. But Pearl had just started playing with us yesterday. If I passed to her, I didn't know for sure if she'd score. I *knew* what *my* feet could do.

So I kept the ball close, making my way down the field.

Hallie ran up. She shouted something, but I didn't hear it.

I was close enough now. I could make

the shot. So I pulled my right foot back and launched the ball at the goal.

Smack! The boy who'd been guarding me stomped his foot in to steal the ball, then passed it to a teammate.

"Get the ball!" Hallie shouted to Ella. But Ella wasn't fast enough. The other team slammed the ball into their goal just as the recess bell buzzed.

Pearl stomped over. She tossed her long blond ponytail over a shoulder. "Why didn't you pass me the ball?"

I shrugged. "I wanted to make sure we won."

"Ugh!" Pearl threw up her hands. "Well, we lost. You're the worst teammate ever, Astrid!"

As Pearl ran back across the blacktop, Hallie caught up to me. "Veejay said he'd take the ball back." She frowned at me. "What's wrong?"

I was still staring after Pearl. I wasn't a bad teammate. I'd just wanted us to win. And that was a good thing, right?

My sweatshirt suddenly felt way too hot. I fluffed my ponytail over my neck to cool off.

"Can we stop for a sec?" I asked. At the edge of the field, I yanked my sweatshirt up over my head.

Pop went my right hearing aid, flying off my ear.

"Oh no!" I shouted.

"I see it!" Hallie said. "It's by the tree."

We stepped closer to look. And yep—a sparkly blue hearing aid sat in the dirt. I picked it up, wiping the earmold off on my shirt.

"Hey, look!" Hallie pointed. A tuft of soft brown fur wiggled into a hole near the roots of the tree.

"It's a baby bunny!" I gasped. Two tiny, furry noses poked out.

"A whole nest of them!" Hallie squealed.

The blacktop was mostly empty now. "We'd better go," I said, fitting the hearing aid back in my ear.

As we jogged back to class, Pearl's words sat like a lump of sticky oatmeal in my stomach. Astronauts were great at teamwork, and I was going to be an astronaut one day. So either I wasn't good enough, or Pearl was wrong. And

I was *definitely* good enough. I had a long way to go, sure, but I worked hard in school. I was good at math. I was in Shooting Stars, our after-school, space-themed club. And I was going to find a way to go to Space Camp this summer. Which meant Pearl was wrong. Anyway, I'd wanted us to win, so I was a *great* teammate. Pearl was the problem.

At least I didn't have to work with her in Shooting Stars.

CHAPTER 2

THE BEST SURPRISE EVER

When I got to the Shooting Stars meeting after school, it looked like it had doubled in size! Blinking at all the new faces, I turned my hearing aids down. It was exciting, but the noise was too much.

Pearl sat in her usual spot, near the door. When our eyes met, she looked away fast.

I squeezed through the crowd. Ms. Ruiz, the

teacher who led Shooting Stars, was talking with another teacher. I tapped her elbow, holding out the small pouch with my clip-on mic in it.

"Great. Thanks, Astrid." Ms. Ruiz clipped the mic to her shirt.

The other teacher grinned at me, like she knew a secret. Her frizzy gray hair was pulled back into a bun, but lots of hairs were trying to escape.

"Why are there so many people here?" I asked Ms. Ruiz. I almost had to shout.

But it was the other teacher who winked at me. "Oh, you'll find out, honey pie."

"Astrid!" someone shouted. (Actually, it sounded more like "aaah—rid," but that was just how my name sounded from far away. My hearing aids worked best up close.)

Before I could turn, I was hug-tackled.

"Hallie?!" I gasped. "You're supposed to be in Petite Picassos."

She grinned. "I am. Mrs. T. told all of us to follow her here."

"'Mrs. T.'?"

"Yeah." Hallie pointed to the woman with curly gray hair. "The art teacher. She teaches Petite Picassos."

So all these extra kids were from the art club? Now I was *really* confused.

"Huh. Well . . . I'm so glad you're here!" I grabbed Hallie's hand and led her over to my table. We squeezed in with Veejay, Ella, and Dominic—and a few new kids who must've been from Petite Picassos.

"All right, let's get started!" called Ms. Ruiz. Her voice was nice and clear through

my hearing aids, thanks to the clip-on mic. "Shooting Stars, you may have noticed that we have a few guests with us today."

We all giggled. "A few" was really "a lot."

"For those new faces, my name is Ms. Ruiz."

"And my name is Mrs. Taggenbottem," said the art teacher. "But all the kids just call me Mrs. T., so you can too." She winked at us. "We have some exciting news for all you little sprouts."

Ms. Ruiz clapped her hands. "Shooting Stars and Petite Picassos will be teaming up for two big projects. For the next month, we'll be doing a STEM project and an art project together."

Hallie and I squealed. We'd get to be together for a whole month!

"For the STEM project, we'll be doing hydroponics," said Ms. Ruiz.

I shot my hand in the air, and Ms. Ruiz

nodded at me. "What's hydro … hydro … ?"

"Great question, Astrid," said Ms. Ruiz. "'Hydroponics' means growing plants without soil. In space, astronauts don't have any dirt, so they grow plants in water instead."

My jaw dropped. How would we do that?

"And for those of you in Shooting Stars," Ms. Ruiz continued, "the hydroponics will count as an Astro Mission. Four points possible."

My eyes bugged out. Four points was a *lot*.

Next to me, Hallie's hand shot up. "What's the art project?"

Mrs. T.'s eyes twinkled. "I'll tell you soon enough. But you'll be working in the same groups for both projects."

"Now for the fun!" Ms. Ruiz pulled out her tablet. "To help both clubs learn from each other, we've decided to assign groups."

Assigned groups?

Hallie and I squeezed each other's hands. Veejay chewed his pencil. Dominic pretended to faint at the idea of us all not being a team.

The teachers began calling names. Stools scraped the floor as kids got up to change seats.

"They're really mixing us up," I said to Hallie. "I thought we'd be together."

Veejay leaned in, pointing to the Astro Board. "Astrid, we could pull into the lead if we both get full points!" He shrugged. "Well, if Pearl doesn't get any."

I studied the giant grid at the back of the STEM lab. Pearl was in first place. In the last Astro Mission, she'd gotten the fastest time on the astronaut-training obstacle course. The one before that, Ms. Ruiz had said her model of the solar system was "perfect." The kid with the most points at the end of the school year would get a scholarship to Space Camp. I *had* to win it. It was the only way my parents would let me go. But I wanted Veejay to go too. Right now, we were tied for second.

"What if we split the scholarship?" Veejay whispered. "If either one of us gets it, we split it?"

"So we can both go." I nodded. "I think my parents would pay for half. If I had a scholarship for the rest."

Veejay grinned. "We'd better work hard to win this thing, then."

"Earth to Veejay!" Ms. Ruiz called. "You're with Chantal, Matt, and Teresa."

He swallowed. "Well, good luck, Astrid." He grabbed his bag and moved across the room.

Hallie gripped my hand harder.

Ms. Ruiz nodded to us. "Astrid, Hallie. You two will be with..." As she scanned her tablet, Hallie and I squealed to each other.

"We get to be together!" I whispered.

"I know!" She grinned back.

"Let's see.... Oh yes." Ms. Ruiz straightened. "You'll be with Jessica from Petite Picassos... and Pearl from Shooting Stars." She waved across the room.

Wait... did she say *Pearl*?

"Oh yay! We already know Pearl. But—" Hallie frowned. "Jessica's visiting family in Brazil for a month. Mrs. T. said so last week."

Ms. Ruiz frowned, tapping on her tablet. "Hmm. You're right. Well, looks like you'll be a team of three."

Pearl perched on an empty stool. She kept

her backpack on her lap, slumping over it. She didn't want to work with us either.

She waited for Ms. Ruiz to leave, then sat up straight. "Just so you know, Astrid—I'm still going to win the scholarship. Even if I have to work with *you*."

I glared back. "We'll see about that." I'd heard it in a movie once. It sounded nice and tough.

Hallie blinked, looking between us. "Um . . . but . . . this is going to be *fun*, right? Guys?"

Yeah, I thought. *About as fun as a papercut.*

But I stretched my mouth into a smile. I'd show Pearl—I was a *fantastic* teammate.

CHAPTER 3
MISSION: CONTROL

"Okay," I said, reading the directions for the hydroponics. "The coconut fiber chunks go into the holes in the Styrofoam."

I reached for the box Ms. Ruiz had given us. Around the room, other teams were starting their plants too. Ms. Ruiz had turned the back area into a grow lab, with plant lights and everything.

Hallie beat me to the box. She frowned, pinching one of the small brown cubes. It looked like dried grass, but harder and browner.

"Be careful," I said, snatching it away.

Hallie shrugged. "What are these for?"

"It's so the roots have something to grab on to," Pearl said. "We put them in the Styrofoam sheet and then float the foam in the tray." She grabbed the foam sheet away from me, holding it up in the air to show Hallie.

"Hey!" I said, grabbing it back. I plopped it in the tray I'd filled with water.

"Well, you haven't let *us* do anything, Astrid." Pearl folded her arms. "This is just like when we play at recess. You're a ball hog and a plant hog."

My cheeks heated. "I am not. Anyway, how would you know? You've only played with us for two days. I pass the ball, right, Hallie?"

But Hallie didn't answer. She reached for a baggie. "Um . . . the seeds are next, right?"

I made myself not grab them from her. I'd prove I wasn't a ball hog—or a plant hog.

One seed for each cube—that's what the sheet said. But I kept my mouth shut as Hallie sprinkled a few over each one.

I glanced up at the Astro Board. Veejay and I were *so close* to first. And growing plants had to be, like, the easiest Astro Mission ever. Even a few extra seeds wouldn't mess things up. Right?

Pearl smirked. "You know, really, if we don't get any points on this, it only matters for you."

I frowned. "What do you mean?"

"Well, it doesn't matter to Hallie, because she's not in Shooting Stars. She's not on the

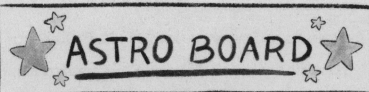

ASTRO BOARD

ASTRID	★	★	★	★	★	★	★	★
VEEJAY	★	★	★	★	★	★	★	
PEARL	★	★	★	★	★	★		
NOA	★	★	★	★	★	★	★	
ELLA	★	★	★	★				
DOMINIC	★	★	★	★	★	★	★	
PRIYA	★	★	★	★	★	★		
CORAL	★	★	★	★	★			
MADDIE	★	★	★	★				
FINN	★	★	★	★	★	★		
JAMAL	★	★	★	★	★	★		
ZEKE	★	★	★	★	★	★		
RISHI	★	★	★	★				
ERIC C.	★	★	★	★	★			
ERIC Z.	★	★	★	★	★	★		
LUZ	★	★	★	★	★			
HANH	★	★	★	★	★	★		
DANIEL	★	★	★	★	★			
IVAN	★	★	★	★				
PETRA	★	★	★					
CARLOS	★	★	★	★	★	★	★	
JESSE	★	★	★	★				
SARAH	★	★	★	★	★			
KEZIAH	★	★	★	★	★	★		
MAX	★	★	★	★	★			

Astro Board. And you and I are on the same team. So we'll get the same points, win or lose. You can't beat me at this."

I swallowed. She was right.

"So maybe we should just let you do the whole thing," she continued. "You seem like you want to, anyway. I might 'accidentally' make a mistake, you know."

My mouth went dry. Was she making a threat?

"All right, class," Ms. Ruiz's voice rang through my hearing aids. "There will be more to do after they sprout in a few days. But for now, we wait. As soon as you finish setting up, hop back over to your tables. Mrs. T. will tell you what to do for the art project."

Hallie did a little dance. "Yay! I wonder what we'll be doing for the art part."

Pearl shrugged. "We're done, aren't we? Let's go."

"Sure. Be there in a sec." As soon as they left, I picked out a few of the extra seeds.

Why was Pearl being so mean about all this? She didn't want to work with me. Well, that was fine. I didn't want to work with her, either. But we still had to. Would she really hurt the plants just because she didn't like me?

"Your group art project only has two rules." Mrs. T. waved her arms like a fairy godmother.

I sat up straighter. Rules were good. And only two? This should be easy!

Next to me, Hallie grinned. Pearl looked bored.

"The first rule is that it must be space-themed."

Space was good. I loved space.

"And the second is this: find a way to mix *reality* with *whimsy*. Petite Picassos, you know what I mean." She winked, then pointed to the middle of the room. "You may use whatever you find on the art cart. You'll have all month for this, so make it good. Don't forget to work together. Go!"

The STEM lab came alive. Kids dashed for the cart, chattering with their teams.

"This is great!" I said to Hallie and Pearl. "You could draw AstroCat, Hallie. You're so good at her."

· "Thanks!" Hallie beamed. "But I don't know..."

Pearl leaned forward. "What does she mean by 'whimsy'?"

"Oh, that's, like, Mrs. T.'s favorite word." Hallie giggled. "It means something you don't expect. We've been doing these in Petite Picassos. Like, you might draw a brush, but instead of bristles, you draw noodles. Or a glass of water, but you put the whole ocean inside."

I scrunched up my nose. "Weird."

Hallie shrugged. "People expect one thing, but you swap it with something else."

"Huh," Pearl said. "That's cool."

Hallie nodded. "So what space-y thing should we do?"

"I know!" I said. "The solar system!"

To my surprise, Pearl nodded.

"Ooh, yeah," Hallie said. "Planets are spheres. We could do a lot with that."

"Like what?" asked Pearl.

I thought hard. "Well . . . we could draw them a lot closer than they really are."

"I don't think that's enough 'whimsy,'" Pearl said.

"Yes, it is." I folded my arms. "The planets are really far apart. We could make them, like, right next to each other."

Hallie shifted. "Well . . . I like the idea of the planets, but . . . I think they need to *be* something."

"They are," I said. "They're the planets."

Pearl sat up straight. "Ooh . . . I've got it! Make them soccer balls! We could have kids kicking balls around in a field, except the balls are the planets!"

Hallie's face lit up. "That's perfect!"

I frowned. My best friend wasn't supposed to be agreeing with Pearl.

"But that doesn't make sense," I said.

"That's the point!" Hallie said.

"Well, I think we should just do the planets," I said.

Pearl's eyes narrowed. "Let's vote. All

in favor of *Soccer System*, raise your hand."
She put her hand in the air.

"That's the perfect name! I love it!" Hallie
glanced at me, and her enthusiasm died. She
slowly raised her hand too. "Sorry, Astrid. It's
a really good idea."

"Well, that's it, then. Two to one." Pearl
smirked at me. "If you get the hydroponics, we
get the art."

What did she mean by that? We were *all*
supposed to do both. I opened my mouth to
ask, but they weren't looking at me anymore.

"What supplies should we use?" Hallie
asked, bouncing in her seat.

As they talked about oil paints and pastels
and other things I'd never heard of, I bit my lip.

Why did Ms. Ruiz have to assign us groups,
anyway? I watched Veejay laughing with his

group. Across the room, Ella was talking with hers. Dominic was clowning around, and his group was laughing.

How were we supposed to be a team if they wouldn't listen to me?

CHAPTER 4

SPROUTS

I pulled the brush across the wall. The paint made a dark blue stripe on the white.

"We make a great team, Petersons," Dad said. He refilled a pan with a sea of dark blue paint.

My big sister, Stella, dragged her roller back and forth. "Our room is going to look so epic, Astrid!"

"I can't wait to add stars." I painted careful lines like Mom had shown us. "What are you going to put on your side?"

"I don't know yet," Stella said. "Maybe some old circuit boards."

"Circuit boards?" I wrinkled my nose. "That's not art."

"Says who? I saw it on a website. It looked cool."

"You'd get along great with Pearl, then," I muttered. I couldn't make myself say, *and Hallie*.

"Who?"

"Just a girl in Shooting Stars." I explained the projects we were doing. I'd checked on our plants twice last week. Two teeny, tiny sprouts had poked their heads out of their shells. But I still didn't know what to do about the art.

"They just didn't get my idea," I said.

"You should draw it," Mom said, straightening the drop cloth. "You know, just a quick sketch. So they can see what you're talking about."

"I don't know," Stella said. "*Soccer System* sounds like a pretty cool id—" She glanced at my face and stopped. "I mean, yeah. Sure. What Mom said."

I nodded, thinking. Who said only Pearl and Hallie got to be in charge of the art project? I was part of the team too.

Maybe Mom was right. If I couldn't explain what I meant with the planet art, maybe a sketch would help. A good teammate made sure their ideas were clear.

☆　☆　☆

On Monday after school, we all squeezed into the plant area in the STEM lab.

"They sprouted!" Hallie squealed.

Of course, I'd already seen them. But they were bigger now. They were still small—but they looked more like lettuce leaves.

"Wow." I ran a finger gently down a leaf.

"Now that they've sprouted, we need to add nutrients," Ms. Ruiz said. "Where do plants normally get their nutrients?" She raised her eyebrows, waiting.

My hand shot in the air. "Soil!"

"Bingo." Ms. Ruiz winked at me. "And since

we're not using soil, we have to add the nutrients to the *water*. This will help the plants grow well."

"What are *nutrients*?" Hallie whispered.

Pearl answered before I could. "They're like vitamins."

Ms. Ruiz was filling little cups with something from a bottle. She held a cup out to us, and Pearl grabbed it.

I scowled. What had happened to Pearl "not caring" about the hydroponics project?

But then I thought of something. What if she wasn't planning to add the nutrients at all? Then our plants wouldn't grow well.

"Maybe I should pour it," I said.

Pearl glared at me. She moved the cup away, and the liquid almost sloshed over the edge. "Why?"

Hallie bit her lip, glancing between us.

"Fine. I'll lift up the Styrofoam," I said. *And watch every move you make.*

Pearl stepped closer to pour. But she tripped over my foot, and the liquid splashed onto the counter.

"Look what you did!" I shouted.

"It was an accident!" Pearl's cheeks were turning red.

Ms. Ruiz hurried over. "Girls, what's the problem?"

I pointed. "Pearl spilled it."

"I tripped," snarled Pearl.

"No worries," Ms. Ruiz said. "You know where we keep rags for spills. And here's another cup." She moved to talk to the whole class. "Once you've added your nutrients, check the pH level. Use the pH meter at your station."

"Oh, pH?" said Hallie. "Like in the lab we did in STEM class."

Pearl tipped the new cup into the water. I made sure she knew I was watching.

From the group next to us, Dominic leaned over. "Our class doesn't have STEM till tomorrow. What's pH?"

"It's how acidic something is," I said. I grabbed the pH meter. "You stick it in the water and press the button."

"Why does it matter?" he asked.

"Uh . . ." I wracked my brain, but I couldn't remember what Ms. Ruiz had said.

But she poked her head in as she passed. "Lettuce grows best in water with a pH of about 6.0," Ms. Ruiz said. "If your pH is below that, it's too acidic. You'll want to add baking soda." She pointed to a box on the counter. "If your pH is above that, it's too basic, and you should add vinegar." She pointed to a plastic bottle. "But not too much of either one!"

"Can I do it?" Hallie asked.

"Sure, Hallie." I smirked at Pearl. *See? I'm not a plant hog.* I handed Hallie the pH meter, and she put it in the water. The screen said 6.0.

"Wow. Perfect!" said Pearl.

"After you clean up, you can work on your art," Ms. Ruiz told us. "Pick one of you to check your pH level this week. One or two checks should be fine."

Had Pearl spilled the nutrients on purpose? Was she planning to do worse once she was alone with the plants?

"I'll do it," I said as soon as Ms. Ruiz was gone.

Hallie nodded. "Okay."

"Fine," Pearl muttered.

On the way back to our lab table, I took a deep breath. "So . . . I drew the planets over the weekend." After painting our bedroom, I'd pulled out *Tour the Solar System*. It was a big book with lots of pictures that I'd gotten for Christmas. I'd spent hours copying Saturn's rings and Jupiter's wavy lines. I pulled my drawing out of my backpack and held it out. "What do you think?"

Hallie and Pearl blinked.

"That's not what we're doing." Pearl pointed at my planets. "We voted."

"I just thought—"

"But the drawings are really good, Astrid." Hallie took the paper. "These are great!"

I blinked. "Really?"

"Yes! I love them."

"I wanted to show you guys what I was trying to say," I said. "That we could just draw the planets all close together. That's enough whisty . . . whimmy . . . whatsy."

"Whimsy," Pearl said. "And that is *not* what we agreed on, Astrid. We're doing *Soccer System.*"

"Ooh, I know!" squealed Hallie. "We could cut these out and glue them on the other paper as the soccer balls! That would look so good!"

I snatched the paper back. "That's not what I meant," I snapped.

Hallie's face fell.

Pearl nudged her. "Come on, let's just start on the field. We'll figure out the planets later. You want to use watercolors?"

"What? Um, yeah. Sure."

As they set up, I swallowed. Even my sketch hadn't convinced them. And now I'd hurt Hallie's feelings. This group project was turning into a group disaster.

CHAPTER 5

PROBLEMS WITH PEARL

"Astrid, are you coming?" Hallie tossed the ball up and caught it. "We're playing soccer again."

Kids shrieked around us, racing to get the gaga ball pit or the best swings.

Ella, Dominic, and a few other kids waved from the field.

I was about to say yes. But then, down the

hall, Ms. Ruiz stepped out of the STEM lab with her coffee mug. She'd left the door open.

"In a sec," I told Hallie. "I'm going to check the plants."

"Come soon. We need you!" As Hallie took off toward the field, I slipped inside the STEM lab.

I tiptoed through the dark. On the other side of the room divider, I blinked at the bright grow lights in the plant area.

"Aaaah!"

Who was that?

Pearl jumped. She shoved something into her pocket.

I folded my arms. "What are you doing here?"

She glanced at the storeroom door. Was she looking for a place to hide?

Suspicious.

She swallowed. "I . . . was just looking for Ms. Ruiz."

"She left." I put my hands on my hips. "And the plants are my job this week."

Pearl backed away from the tray. "Well, I'm not stopping you."

"Okay," I said.

"Okay." Pearl's eyes flicked again to the storeroom door. Then she bolted out of the lab.

Very suspicious.

Carefully lifting the foam, I stuck the pH meter into the water. A number lit up: 5.7.

What?!

I tested it again to make sure. It was too low! Maybe Pearl *had* done something to the water. I didn't want to believe she'd really do that, but . . .

I checked the chart Ms. Ruiz had put up on

the wall. It was less than 6.0, which meant the water was too acidic. So . . . I should add baking soda.

Biting my lip, I shook a little of the white powder into the water. Was that enough? Ms. Ruiz had said only a little, but what if Pearl came back and added more of whatever she'd put in? I shook more in, just in case. It was kind of clumpy. I shook the box harder to get it out.

Plop! A giant glob bounced into the water.

Gulp.

I put the box back and dashed out to the soccer field.

At least Pearl hadn't been there to see my mistake. Hopefully it wouldn't be a big deal.

☆　☆　☆

A week later at Shooting Stars, Ms. Ruiz clipped my mic to her collar. "Your plants don't need you today. So . . . we thought we'd give you the whole time to work on your art." Next to her, Mrs. T. beamed.

Lots of kids cheered. I groaned, slumping on the table.

"I'll get the paints." Pearl shot out of her seat.

Hallie pulled out the paper they'd been painting on. "What do you think so far, Astrid?"

I didn't answer. I was watching Pearl, because she hadn't gone to get the paints. Instead, she'd gone back into the plant area.

"Astrid?" Hallie waved a hand in front of my face.

"Right. Sorry."

Hallie had sketched the outlines of kids in soccer clothes. One was really close up, about to kick a ball that she hadn't added yet. Pearl had been painting some trees in the back-ground. She'd even added a little bunny—just like the ones we'd found at the edge of the field.

I blinked a few times. It looked . . . really cool.

But planets would look silly once they added them. They didn't go with soccer.

"It's . . ." I swallowed, reminding myself to be nice. Hallie had worked hard on this.

"I like your drawings," I said, and meant it.

"Thanks." Hallie smiled.

Pearl came out from the back. She was headed for the art cart.

"Look!" I whispered to Hallie. "Pearl was back by the plants!"

Hallie frowned. "So? Maybe she got a drink of water."

I pointed to the water bottle sticking out of Pearl's backpack. "Nope. I think she's trying to hurt our plants. I think she spilled the nutrients on purpose. And—"

"Why would she do that?"

I was about to answer when Pearl plopped the paints down in front of us.

Ms. Ruiz came up right behind her. "So what are you guys working on? I can't wait to see!"

I'd have to talk to Hallie later.

Hallie beamed at her. "It's a soccer field. Kids are going to be kicking around the planets as if they're soccer balls!"

I leaned back so she could get a good look. Ms. Ruiz would back me up. She knew tons about space.

But she gasped. "What a creative idea! I love it." She waved Mrs. T. over to look too.

Maybe I hadn't heard her right.

"We know it's not the way planets really are, though," I blurted out. "I mean, planets don't belong on a soccer field."

"That's the whole point of the project, Astrid." Ms. Ruiz's eyes sparkled. "To work together to create something that's surprising."

Hallie nodded. "And Astrid drew some really good planets."

"Did she now?" Mrs. T. said as she joined us.

My cheeks warmed. "We're still deciding what to use for the planets."

"Hmm." Mrs. T. smiled at us. "Well, I'm sure you darlings will figure it out. Wonderful work so far."

Mrs. T. and Ms. Ruiz left to check on other students.

"Are you sure we can't use your planets, Astrid?" Hallie asked.

I folded my arms. "No. They were for something else." *Like the project we* should *be doing.*

"Fine." Pearl tossed her ponytail. "Then here. You didn't do anything last time. You can help with the grass today." She shoved a paintbrush into my hand.

Hallie looked uncomfortable.

But I took the brush. "Fine."

As I made tons of tiny green lines, I wondered what Pearl had been doing back by the plants. Hallie was doing pH checks this week. So it wasn't Pearl's turn.

But for now, I kept my mouth closed and kept painting the grass.

CHAPTER 6

CIRCUIT BOARDS AND SOCCER BALLS

"Can you pass the hammer?" Stella asked, holding a nail against the wall.

Dad grabbed it before I could. "Here you go."

Mom sat next to me on my new bedspread. She flipped pages in an old calendar. She pointed to a picture of hundreds of galaxies. They looked like tiny disks of glitter. "Ooh . . . what about this one, Astrid?"

Our walls were done—they were a perfect, space-y blue. I'd added a few stars on my side. We'd moved the beds and stuff in yesterday. Now Mom and Dad were helping us decorate.

"I love it!" I told Mom. "What are you hanging, Stella?"

"Circuit boards!" she said, holding a second nail in her mouth. *Thunk, thunk,* went the hammer.

"I still don't think those are art," I said. I held up the next page in the calendar for her. "Are you sure you don't want the Milky Way?"

"Art is a matter of opinion, Astrogirl." Dad winked at me.

I rolled my eyes. Mom and I kept sorting through the photos. We tore out a couple of my favorites. Mom said she'd put them in some frames we'd gotten at a thrift store.

"And we're saving a frame for AstroCat, right?" I held up the picture Hallie had drawn for me. It had hung above my bed for the last two years.

"You bet."

I looked up just as Stella hung the last circuit board, and my jaw dropped. She'd fitted them together in a neat grid. Colorful wires connected them.

"That's . . . amazing," I breathed. I stood up to get a better look.

"Thanks!" Stella beamed.

"Do the circuits do anything?"

"Nope." Stella stepped back to survey her work. "They're just pretty."

And they were. Circuit boards weren't supposed to hang on a wall or be pretty, but . . . this looked *really* cool.

Dad closed up the box of nails. "The *unexpected* makes for the best art."

I chewed my lip. Planets as soccer balls were unexpected too. The idea hadn't sounded like a good one, but once I'd seen it . . . well, it had looked good. I guess I'd just felt like science and art were two different things and should stay that way. But maybe I was wrong.

Well . . . Pearl might have had an okay idea about the art, but did she have to be so mean about it? And we still didn't know what she was doing to the plants. Hallie wasn't even worried about it.

I had to catch Pearl. If I had proof, Hallie would believe me. And so would Ms. Ruiz.

It was time to make sure I got full points on this Astro Mission.

CHAPTER 7

SOMETHING SMELLS

Hallie shrugged. "Maybe they moved?"

We peered into the bunny burrow. It was empty. Tiny bits of fluff clung to the sides.

"Do bunnies do that?"

It was Monday. I was determined to keep an eye on Pearl. I'd convinced Hallie to play on the blacktop today—the field was too far away from the STEM lab. Friday was the last day of the Astro Mission; I didn't have much time left.

Hallie giggled. "What if a bunny-sized moving truck came to help them?"

"That would be funny." I grinned, thinking of a tiny truck filled with carrots. "Hey, how were the plants last week?"

Hallie's eyes darted around. "Um . . . they were . . . fine."

"Hallie?"

She smiled, but it wasn't very convincing.

"Did you forget to check on them last week?"

She paused, then hung her head. "Yeah."

"It's okay," I said, sighing. "It's only been a week. We'll check on them today."

☆   ☆   ☆

"Something smells." Dominic pinched his nose as we all crowded into the STEM lab after school. Other kids fanned the air or said, "Ew."

And they were right.

We all rushed back to the plants to make sure it wasn't ours that stank.

But it was coming from *our* plants.

Pearl wrinkled her nose. "Are they supposed to be all yellow and shriveled?"

Ms. Ruiz hurried over. "Hmm," she said. She lifted up the foam and sniffed at the roots, which were yellow, too. "Root rot. And phew!" She fanned the air. "Someone's been adding too much vinegar!"

I glared at Pearl. "We should check the pH."

"Good call, Astrid." Ms. Ruiz stuck the pH meter in and pressed the button. It was 3.8!

"How did that happen?!" shouted Pearl.

I put my hands on my hips. "You've been doing something to the water. I saw you."

The room got quiet as kids turned to stare.

Pearl's face went red. "No, I didn't. I told you—I was just checking on them. It was your job to add stuff that week, and Hallie's job last week!"

"You told me you were looking for Ms. Ruiz," I said.

Ms. Ruiz turned to Pearl. "Well, mistakes happen. I've seen you in here a few times over the last week, Pearl. Were you checking on the plants all those times?"

I blinked. She'd been in here *more* times?

Pearl swallowed. "I . . . uh . . . yeah. I was just checking on the plants. What's wrong with that?"

Ms. Ruiz shook her head. "You three need to start communicating better. For now, change this water. You can still save your plants."

We nodded. The other kids went back to their own projects.

"Guys, I didn't do anything to the plants. I promise," Pearl said after Ms. Ruiz left.

"You were the one who said you didn't care about this Astro Mission," I said.

Pearl crossed her arms. "I never said that. I just said I didn't need the points to beat you."

"It sounds the same to me."

"I shouldn't have said it, okay?" She sniffed. "I'm sorry."

"But I saw you in here," I said. "You had something in your pocket."

"Well, it's not what you think."

I put my hands on my hips. "Then what was it?"

"None of your business." She glared at me.

Hallie pushed between us. "Guys! Are you going to keep fighting, or are we going to save our plants?" She picked up the tray.

I jumped in to help her carry it, and Pearl grabbed the bottle of plant nutrients. As we carried it all over to the sink, I watched Pearl. She seemed like she was telling the truth. But if she wasn't hurting the plants, why else had she been in here?

CHAPTER 8

SPYING

Later in the week, I crouched behind a cupboard in the STEM lab. I'd spent recesses here for the last two days. It was Pearl's week to check on the plants—the perfect time for her to do something to them. So I was going to catch her.

I'd hidden my clip-on mic near our plants. That way, I'd be able to hear anything Pearl said, even from behind the cupboard.

It was really dusty back here. I was pretty sure there was a dead spider in the corner. But I took a deep breath. I had to save our plants. And I had to find out for sure if Pearl was hurting them.

Just as I was about to sneeze, somebody tiptoed into the plant area.

I clamped a hand over my nose and sucked myself back.

"Okay, little plants. *Think green.*" The words came through my hidden mic. Someone was right next to our plants!

When I was sure I wasn't going to sneeze, I slowly peeked out.

Oh—it was just Hallie.

I crept out. "Hey, Hallie."

She jumped, dropping something. "Astrid!

I'm—I'm sorry. I'm so sorry—" She picked up what she'd dropped. It was ... a *green marker*?

I frowned. "What are you doing?"

"It's my fault. I think I killed our plants!"

My eyes widened. "Did you *color* them?"

"No—I was going to. I thought it would help them look healthy. This project is a big deal for you. I want you to be able to go to Space Camp. You were so worried about getting everything just right, and I was scared I'd mess it up for you."

My stomach tightened. I'd made Hallie scared, and she just wanted to be a good friend to me. I bit my lip. "I guess I was a little bossy, huh?"

"Maybe a little," she said.

And if I'd been bossy with Hallie, I'd been bossy with Pearl.

But Pearl deserved it, I thought. *She called me a plant hog.*

But maybe... maybe I *had* been a plant hog.

Hallie's shoulders fell. "It's all my fault."

I shook my head. "Just because you forgot to check on them last week?"

She sniffled. "But I *did* check on them," she said. "The pH was really high—7.5."

Too *high*? I swallowed. That would've been right after . . . after I added the baking soda.

That giant clump *had* been too much.

"So I added vinegar, like the chart says." Hallie pointed above us. "But I added too much. It's why the pH was so low when Ms. Ruiz measured it. It's why the plants were stinky."

"Why did you tell me you forgot?"

Hallie shrugged. "Because I knew I messed up. I didn't want you to be mad. I thought maybe I could fix it today with the marker."

I took a deep breath. "It's not your fault. I put in too much baking soda. I was worried Pearl was adding something to the water, so I tried to make up for it."

"Is that why you were spying?"

I nodded. "I wanted to catch her."

Hallie gave a nervous laugh. "And the whole time, it was us."

I giggled. "Ms. Ruiz was right. We needed to be a better team. Our poor plants."

Hallie smiled. "Still friends?"

"Friends forever."

Hallie tapped her chin. "But if it was us, then what *was* Pearl doing in here? I think she was telling the truth when she said she didn't do anything to them."

"I don't kn—"

But Hallie's eyes flicked toward the door. She put a finger to her lips.

Someone was coming.

I pulled Hallie back to my hiding spot. We slipped behind the cupboard just in time.

Pearl was tiptoeing over to our plants.

CHAPTER 9

PEARL'S SECRET

Pearl looked our plants over. She took a deep breath. "One leaf," she whispered. Like with Hallie, I heard it thanks to the mic I'd hidden.

Hallie raised an eyebrow at me. What was Pearl doing?

I shrugged. I had no idea.

Pearl bent closer to the plants. Then she ripped off a leaf of the lettuce!

Hallie started forward, but I pulled her back. *Wait,* I signed. I only knew a few signs, but I'd taught Hallie what I knew. It came in handy.

But then Pearl sighed. "It's not enough." And she tore off a few more leaves.

Hallie pointed, raising her eyebrows. She thought we should stop her.

But if we stopped her, we wouldn't get answers. So I shook my head, putting a finger to my lips.

Pearl looked around to make sure she was alone. Hallie and I slunk farther back into the shadows. We peeked out again just in time to see her open the storeroom door.

We crept out of our hiding spot. As we got closer to the storeroom, there were scratching noises. Pearl was squatting over a box. Her back was to us.

In the doorway, I put my hands on my hips. "I knew you were up to something!"

Pearl turned around so fast, her feet slipped out from under her. And inside the box, a ball of brown fluff munched on the lettuce. The bunny sniffed the air, then went back to its lunch.

Hallie peeked over my shoulder. "You're hiding a *bunny*?"

"Please don't tell anyone," Pearl said.

I knelt to get a better look. "It's one of the bunnies from the field, isn't it?"

She nodded. "It's hurt. I think something attacked them a couple weeks ago. The others were all gone when I got there. I found this one hiding by another tree."

"He's so cute." Hallie made kissing noises at the bunny.

"Why did you keep him in here?" I asked.

"My dad won't let us have pets," Pearl said. "And Ms. Ruiz doesn't use this closet much. I was hoping he could just stay here till he got better, and then I could find him a new home."

"And . . . you fed him our lettuce," I said.

Pearl nodded. "At first, I was giving him lettuce from my lunch. That's what I was hiding when you came in that time. But my mom switched to hummus and pita bread this week. I didn't know where else to get food for him. I'm sorry I did it without asking you guys."

"It's okay with me," Hallie said. "You're doing a nice thing, Pearl."

It *was* nice. But she was breaking about a million rules. I was about to point that out, but the bunny raised his nose at me, sniffing. Like he was asking me for help.

I hadn't been a great teammate to Pearl. And maybe being a good teammate didn't just mean caring about winning. Maybe it meant caring about your team.

Pushing to my feet, I ran back out to our plants.

"Astrid?" Hallie called.

"Please don't tell!" Pearl yelled.

But I came back with my fists full. I dropped the rest of our lettuce in with the bunny.

"You could get in a lot of trouble," I said. "But I think there's a way to help the bunny *and* follow the rules. I want to help. We're a team, after all."

Hallie nodded. "Me too."

And for the first time ever, Pearl actually smiled at me.

CHAPTER 10

PART OF THE TEAM

"Welcome to the last day of both our Astro Mission and our art project!" Ms. Ruiz clapped her hands. We were all squeezed into the plant area.

"It has been so much fun seeing all of you work together." Mrs. T. grinned. "Today, we'll measure our lettuce. Then we'll show off our art and have a lettuce-munching party."

Hallie, Pearl, and I gripped each other's hands.

Ms. Ruiz and Mrs. T. started going around to measure.

"I'm nervous," Pearl breathed.

We stared at the shriveled bits of green and yellow—all that was left of our plants. But I knew that wasn't why Pearl was nervous.

"It'll be okay," I told her. "We're with you."

Hallie nodded.

Ms. Ruiz strode up. My heart fluttered faster as she peered at our plants.

She raised an eyebrow. "Do you three want to tell me anything?"

"Yes," I said. "You and Mrs. T. said the first day that the point of these projects was to learn from one another. We didn't do that very well at first. We made a lot of mistakes."

I glanced at Hallie.

She nodded. "But we got better at it."

"And we have no lettuce left," whispered Pearl. "Because . . ."

"Because we gave it to someone who needed it more." I glanced around to make sure no one else was watching us. "Can we show you something?"

We led a very confused Ms. Ruiz to the storeroom. Hallie clicked on the light.

Pearl pulled the box from its hiding spot.

"Oh my goodness!" Ms. Ruiz exclaimed. The color drained from her face.

I glanced at Hallie. I really hoped Ms. Ruiz wouldn't get angry. It had been my idea to tell her. And my idea for us to tell her together—it would be easier for Pearl.

Ms. Ruiz set aside her tablet and bent over

the bunny. She examined its hurt leg. "Where did you three find him?"

We told her how Pearl had rescued him. Then all about our lettuce and how we'd decided to feed the rest of it to the bunny.

I swallowed. "So…we need help. This bunny needs a safe place to live, and we don't know what to do. We're sorry we kept it a secret."

"Well, it was very wrong to keep it a secret. Pearl, I wish you'd asked for help from the start. I want your help cleaning up after the next three club meetings to make up for it."

Pearl hung her head. "Okay."

"But your heart was in the right place. As a matter of fact, I've been thinking that the STEM lab needs a pet. I'll call the local animal shelter about vaccines and help with his leg. And then, if they give the okay, I'll adopt him."

"For . . . experiments?" Hallie asked.

Ms. Ruiz laughed. "No! As a pet, of course."

Pearl swiped at her eyes, which were red. "Really?"

"Really. But only if you will give the bunny a name."

Pearl grinned. "I can do that."

☆ ☆ ☆

Half an hour later, I sank my teeth into a lettuce leaf. *Crunch.* Veejay's team had gotten full points on the Astro Mission, and they were sharing their lettuce with us. Some kids sat with their art, and some were wandering around chatting.

Ms. Ruiz came over to our table. I had to admit, our art looked great. Hallie had done all the drawing, and Pearl had done most of the painting. I'd cut my planets out, and we'd glued them on. The kid in front was about to kick the planet Earth right at you.

"You three really came together," Ms. Ruiz said. "And even though your lettuce didn't do too well, you made a good decision to ask for help."

Pearl's eyes shone.

Ms. Ruiz took a deep breath. "And that's

why I'm giving you partial credit on the Astro Mission. Two points each."

It was not the full four, but I hadn't expected *any*.

"Thank you!" Pearl and I shouted. Hallie beamed.

"It's for working as a team. Often the *real* Astro Mission." Ms. Ruiz winked at us.

She moved on to talk to the next group, and Pearl slid the art across the table to me. "I think Astrid should get to keep *Soccer System*. Is that okay, Hallie?"

"Good with me," Hallie said.

"Really?" I asked.

Pearl nodded. "Thanks for sticking up for me and the bunny. You were right. Ms. Ruiz fixed it."

"Wow. Thanks!" Mom and I had one frame

left. It would be perfect for *Soccer System*!

"What are you going to name the bunny, Pearl?" asked Hallie.

Pearl grinned. "Well, I think he should join the team, right? So . . . Petite Star? Or Shooting Picasso?"

I giggled. "I don't know if those sound right."

Hallie nodded. "What about something that's both space-y and pretty?"

"Yeah!" I said. "How about a galaxy?"

"I like it," Pearl said, tapping her chin. "Galaxia the Super Space Bunny."

"Perfect!" I said as Hallie and I giggled.

And it was.

AUTHOR'S NOTE

I'm an audiologist who supports access to language—whether it be spoken, signed, or both. I've written Astrid with hearing aids and spoken language because I'm the most familiar with that perspective, but I have great respect for the Deaf community and signed languages like American Sign Language (ASL). There are a lot of great books out there with deaf/hard-of-hearing characters that are written from other perspectives. For a starter list, find my profile on Instagram @rienealwriter.